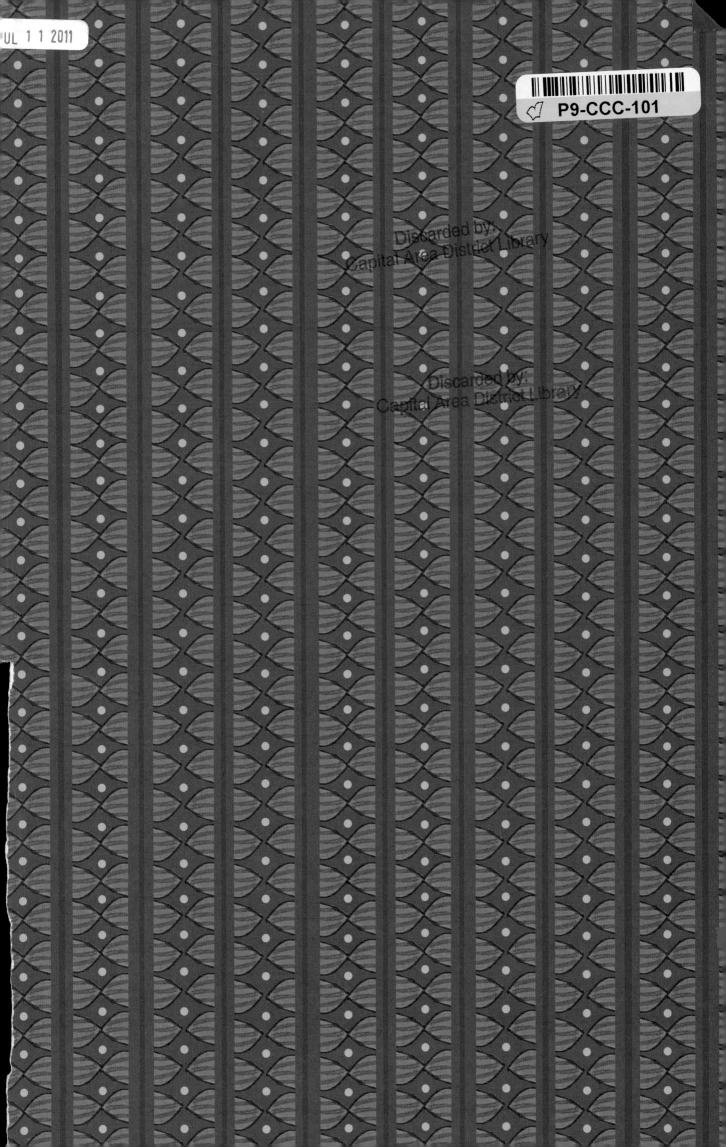

Pussycat,

Pussycat...

For Mimi and Sasha
and Blackie who watches over them both.
— Dan

For Gabor, my beloved life-partner and friend.
and
For my aunt, Mona LaVine (1932-2010) — A traveler and
spiritual seeker, whose kindness gave warmth and
comfort to strangers and friends, all over the world.

— Rae

Published in 2011 by Simply Read Books
www.simplyreadbooks.com

Text © 2011 Dan Bar-el
Illustrations © 2011 Rae Maté

We gratefully acknowledge for their financial support of our
publishing program the Canada Council for the Arts, the BC
Arts Council, and the Government of Canada through the
Book Publishing Industry Development Program (BPIDP).

Manufactured in China   10 9 8 7 6 5 4 3 2 1

Book design by Elisa Gutiérrez

LIBRARY AND ARCHIVES CANADA CATALOGUING IN PUBLICATION

Bar-el, Dan
    Pussycat, Pussycat, where have you been? / written by
Dan Bar-el ; illustrated by Rae Maté.

ISBN 978-1-897476-46-8

    I. Maté, Rae, 1948- II. Title.

PS8553.A76229P88 2011   jC813'.54   C2010-905677-9

Dan Bar-el

Pussycat, Pussycat, where have you been?

illustrations by Rae Maté

Simply Read Books

Pussycat, Pussycat,
Where have you been?

I've been to London
To see the Queen.

Pussycat, Pussycat,
What did you there?

I chased a mouse
From under the chair.

Pussycat, Pussycat,
What did you then?

I went to France
And sailed down the Seine.

Pussycat, Pussycat,
Did you stay long?

Just for the length
Of a toe-tapping song.

Pussycat, Pussycat,
What followed after?

A dream and a breeze,
A night full of laughter.

Pussycat, Pussycat,
How far did you go?

The length of a stage
And the span of a show.

Pussycat, Pussycat,
Where did you stop?

Below the equator,
One step and one hop.

Pussycat, Pussycat,
What did you find?

The strange and peculiar,
The one of a kind.

Pussycat, Pussycat,
Who else did you meet?

The pageant performers
    Along every street.

Pussycat, Pussycat,
Did you join in?

If life is a circus
    Why wait to begin.

Pussycat, Pussycat,
What seas did you course?

The frozen cold water
That lies to the North.

Pussycat, Pussycat,
What did you see?

Pods of gray whales
Swimming so free.

Pussycat, Pussycat,
Where did you stray?

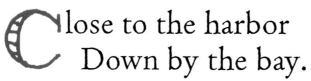lose to the harbor
Down by the bay.

Pussycat, Pussycat,
For what did you wish?

I wished for a fisher
To spare me one fish.

Pussycat, Pussycat,
What touched your heart?

A train whistle moaning
Its way through the dark.

Pussycat, Pussycat,
What stopped your sorrow?

I sang to the stars
As I rode to tomorrow.

Pussycat, Pussycat,
What signs did you follow?

Star charts and riddles
In mountains made hollow.

Pussycat, Pussycat,
Were answers discovered?

For each mystery solved
A thousand stayed covered.

Pussycat, Pussycat,
Where did you sail?

Above the red desert
On old winds that wail.

Pussycat, Pussycat,
What did you hear?

The spirits you dance with
And spirits you fear.

Pussycat, Pussycat,
What was most scary?

Thunder and lightning
That rolled 'cross the Prairies.

Pussycat, Pussycat,
Where did you hide?

In soft golden wheat fields
Where whispers abide.

Pussycat, Pussycat,
Did you get lost?

I strayed from the path
At whatever the cost.

Pussycat, Pussycat,
But were you all right?

The kindness of strangers
Gave warmth to my night.

Pussycat, Pussycat,
What brought you back?

Alone burning candle
Through moonless night's black.

Pussycat, Pussycat,
What kept you brave?

To know you were waiting
Beyond the next wave.

Pussycat, Pussycat,
Will you stay home?

I always get restless,
   I always will roam.

Pussycat, Pussycat,
I'll miss you again.

Then come travel with me,
   My partner, my friend.

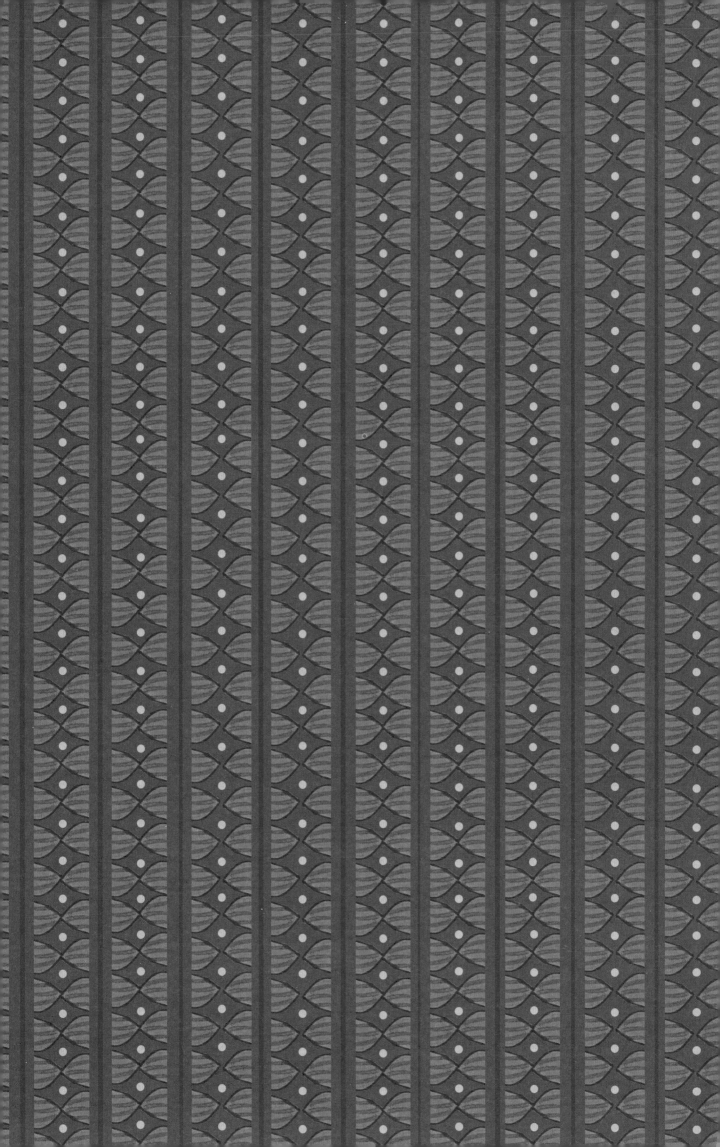